BEARD IN A BOX

BY BILL COTTER

Alfred A. Knopf   New York

My dad is the coolest.

He's also
the tallest,

the fastest,

the strongest.

The awesomest!

After extensive research, I discovered the source of his power . . .

His beard!

The results were conclusive.

It was time I got a
beard of my own.

Introducing . . .

KID-TESTED
DAD-APPROVED!

BEARD IN A BOX

CHOOSE FROM
100s OF STYLES!

THE HIPSTER

THE LINCOLN

THE MOUNTAIN MAN

from SCAM-O! Makers of the Talking Toupee and the Baby Barber Kit

Grow a beard (almost) instantly!

Just follow 5 easy steps . . .

and BAM!
You're in Beardtown, baby!

King of the Scene!

BEARD in a BOX comes with:

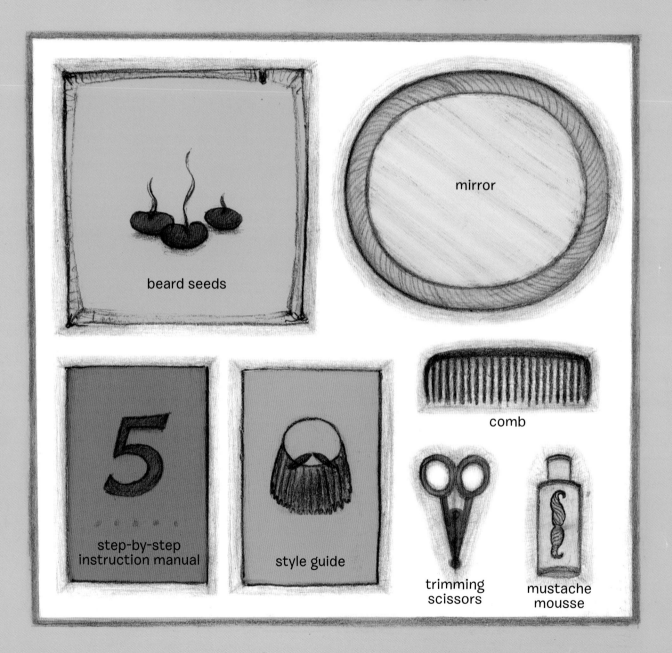

beard seeds

mirror

step-by-step
instruction manual

style guide

comb

trimming
scissors

mustache
mousse

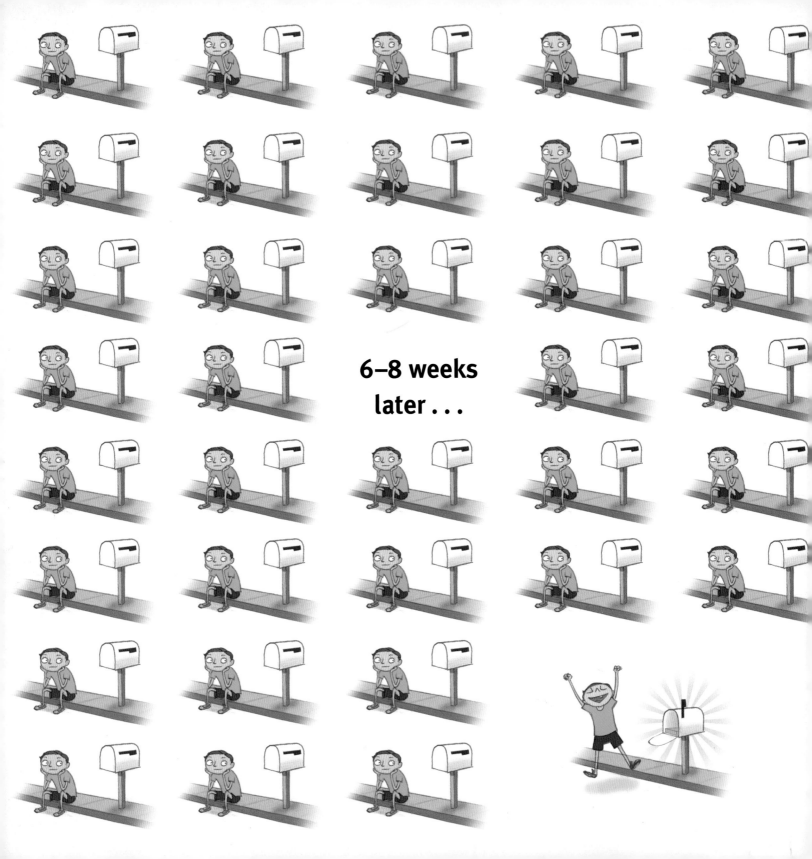

6–8 weeks
later . . .

It was finally here.
I ripped open the box and
started the 5-step program.

Step 1: Choose your style.

the Double-Beard

the Hippie

the Beatnik

the Wizard

the Hipster

the Creep

the Lincoln

the Fu Manchu

the Tycoon

the Mountain Man

the Artist

the Biker

the Goatee

the Octopus

the King Tut

the Santa

Step 2: Apply beard seeds.

Step 3: Water generously.

Step 4: Do face exercises.

Come here, little dude. . . . Awesomeness doesn't have anything to do with beards. It's about the kind of person you are.

You've got to be kidding me!!! This whole time I was trying to get a beard so I'd be awesome like you!

Don't worry. I'll show you.

For Luke and Oliver

THIS IS A BORZOI BOOK PUBLISHED BY ALFRED A. KNOPF

Copyright © 2016 by Bill Cotter

All rights reserved. Published in the United States by Alfred A. Knopf, an imprint of Random House Children's Books, a division of Penguin Random House LLC, New York.

Knopf, Borzoi Books, and the colophon are registered trademarks of Penguin Random House LLC.

Visit us on the Web! randomhousekids.com

Educators and librarians, for a variety of teaching tools, visit us at RHTeachersLibrarians.com

Library of Congress Cataloging-in-Publication Data
Cotter, Bill, author, illustrator.
Beard in a Box / Bill Cotter. — First edition.
p. cm.
Summary: Wanting to be more like his father, a young boy spends all of his money on a product that will supposedly let him grow a beard almost instantly.
ISBN 978-0-553-50835-2 (trade) — ISBN 978-0-553-50836-9 (lib. bdg.) — ISBN 978-0-553-50837-6 (ebook)
[1. Beards—Fiction. 2. Fathers and sons—Fiction. 3. Swindlers and swindling—Fiction.] I. Title.
PZ7.C8289Be 2016   [E]—dc23   2014047471

The illustrations in this book were created using graphite, watercolor, and Adobe Photoshop.

MANUFACTURED IN CHINA   April 2016
10 9 8 7 6 5 4 3 2 1   First Edition